Dancing in Water

Story by Diana Noonan

Illustrations by Nathalie Ortega

Contents

Chapter 1

Skylar Loves Dancing

Skylar loved to dance.

She had been going to ballet classes since she was four years old.

"I like dancing more than anything in the whole world!" Skylar always told her mum.

Skylar liked her colourful dance costumes.

She liked to slip and slide gracefully in time to the music.

She liked to leap up and change direction.

But there was one thing Skylar didn't like about dancing. After class, her ankle *always* hurt.

"We'd better ask Dr Lei about that ankle," said Mum one day, after class.

Mum took Skylar to see Dr Lei.

As soon as Dr Lei looked at Skylar's ankle, Skylar sensed she had some bad news for them.

"I'm afraid your ankle needs at least a year's rest from dancing," said Dr Lei.

Skylar gave a gasp.

"But you can still walk and play and swim," said Dr Lei in a kind, calm voice.

Chapter 2

Ms Puri's Clever Idea

That night, Skylar was miserable.
She felt like crying.

At school the next day, she became so upset
that she really did cry.

"What's the matter, Skylar?" asked her teacher, Ms Puri.

Ms Puri listened carefully as Skylar told her
what Dr Lei had said.

Ms Puri thought for a minute. Then she asked,
"Skylar, can you float, and hold your breath underwater?"

Skylar nodded.

"Then I have an idea," said Ms Puri.
"Come to the pool on Thursday after school.
I think you will like what you see."

Chapter 3

A Different Kind of Dance

When Mum and Skylar arrived at the pool on Thursday, Skylar was surprised to see Ms Puri there. She was coaching a team of older girls in the water.

Skylar liked the girls' colourful swimsuits.

Suddenly, music began to play.
Ms Puri blew her whistle.

Skylar watched in amazement as the team moved around the water in time to the beat of the music.

"This is artistic swimming," said Mum.
"It's a different kind of dancing!"

Skylar watched the girls float and gracefully change direction.

She watched them dive beneath the water,
then leap out of it.

"I think I would enjoy this," she said.

"I'm sure it wouldn't hurt your ankle," replied Mum.
"I'll ask Ms Puri for the phone number of the Under 10s coach."

That night at dinner, Mum had some good news for Skylar.

"I called the Under 10s artistic swimming coach today," she said.
"You can try out for the team next Thursday!"

Skylar was so excited.
That night, she even dreamed
she was a famous Olympic artistic swimmer!

But in the morning, Skylar began to worry.

"What if I can't do the moves?" she asked Mum. "What if I disappoint the coach and don't make the team?"

"I'm sure you will do well," said Mum.

Chapter 4

Skylar in the Water

On Thursday, when Skylar went to the pool,
the coach was waiting to welcome her.
"Hello, Skylar," she said. "My name is Rachel."

Skylar went and put on her swimming gear.

Then, Rachel handed her a nose clip.
"This will help you to hold your breath underwater,"
she said.

Skylar stood at the pool's edge with two other girls who were trying out for the team.

Rachel showed them how to get into the pool gracefully.

Rachel told them how to float, and how to move backwards and forwards in the water.

Then she turned on some music
and asked the girls to move to the beat.

When they had finished,
Rachel called Skylar over to the edge of the pool.
"Have you ever been to dance class?" asked Rachel.

"Yes," replied Skylar. "I've been dancing for four years."

"I see," said Rachel, thoughtfully.

Chapter 5

Still a Dancer

That night in bed, Skylar worried
about getting into the artistic swimming team.

Could I have tried harder? she wondered.

But then she saw Mum at her bedroom door.

"Skylar, guess what?" Mum said.
"Rachel just called to invite you to join the team!
She said that she can tell you're a very good dancer."

Skylar gave a huge grin.

"I'm still going to be a dancer!" she said, jumping out of bed. "But now, I'll be dancing in water!"